# The Dogs

## by

## Mark Morris

## Illustrated by Roy Petrie

First published in 2001 in Great Britain by
Barrington Stoke Ltd, Sandeman House, Trunk's Close,
55 High Street, Edinburgh EH1 1SR
www.barringtonstoke.co.uk

Reprinted 2005

ISBN 1-902260-76-7

Printed in Great Britain by Bell & Bain Ltd

# A Note from the Author

My wife and I once stayed in Kent with a friend of ours called Hilary. Hilary told us that five years earlier she had owned two dogs. She took them for a walk in the country one day, and when the time came to go home, she called them, but they didn't come. She and her friends spent hours looking for them, but couldn't find them anywhere. Hilary never saw her dogs again.

As a writer, I often think *what if*. When Hilary told us this story, I thought to myself, *what if* the dogs were to walk in to the house right now, five years after they'd gone missing, and *what if* they looked exactly the same ...

# Contents

# Chapter 1
# The Police Station, Part 1

Alice Manly couldn't stop shaking. She was sitting in a bare room. The walls were an icy blue. There was very little furniture, just a table and three plastic chairs, two in charcoal-grey, the other in pumpkin-orange.

The police officers sitting across from her seemed kindly enough. The police constable leaning against the wall behind them looked watchful. The woman was sitting on the orange chair opposite Alice. It creaked when she leaned forward to switch on a tape machine set into the wall. Though she looked tired, her voice sounded clear and precise.

"Interview with Alice Jane Manly, commencing at 2:16 a.m., Friday, 26th May 2000. Present in the room is Alice Jane Manly, myself, Detective Inspector Elizabeth Farrington, Detective Sergeant Frank Lockwood and Police Constable Michael Moss." She leaned back in her chair and looked at Alice for a moment. Then she said, "Now then, Alice, do you know why you're here?"

Alice nodded and closed her hands around the plastic tea cup in front of her in the hope that it would stop her shaking. Hot tea slopped over her hand, though she hardly felt it. "Yes," she whispered.

"Is there anything you'd like to tell us?" Farrington asked.

Alice looked up and suddenly the walls seemed too bright, as if sunlight was reflecting off them. She felt sick and dizzy, but she managed to gasp, "Yes. Yes, I want to tell you everything. I want to go right back to when it all began."

# Chapter 2
# Bad News

One day, half her life ago, nine-year-old Alice Manly was sitting in a Religious Education lesson. They were learning about Jesus and the story of the loaves and fishes. It was nearly lunchtime and her stomach was rumbling so loudly that it made her blush. Tim, who sat next to her, had put up his hand and asked Mrs Mason whether

Jesus had had any tomato ketchup to put on the fish. They were all laughing, when there was a knock on the classroom door.

"Come in," Mrs Mason called and a tall girl with plaits walked into the room.

"Miss, is Alice Manly here?" the girl asked.

"Yes, she's here," Mrs Mason replied. "Is she wanted for something?"

The girl nodded. "Mr Gregory wants to see her straight away in his office. He gave me this note to give you."

Alice felt herself blushing as everyone looked at her. Mrs Mason peered at the note and said, "All right, Alice. Off you go then."

Alice followed the tall girl down the corridor. She tried to work out what she'd done wrong. She'd pulled Tasha's hair hard enough to make her cry yesterday, but that was because Tasha had flicked an elastic band at her. A week ago she'd chalked JACKIE FOREMAN LOVES TONY HARDING on the wall outside the gymnasium, but the rain had washed that off a couple of days later.

When Alice went into Mr Gregory's office he was sitting with his hands folded on the desk in front of him. To her surprise she saw that Mrs Pike, Alexa's Mum, was there too, sitting opposite him. Alice had been staying with the Pikes for the past ten days while her parents had been in Hong Kong. Dad had gone there on business and just this once had taken Mum along for a treat.

Alexa's Mum turned towards Alice as she walked in. Alice was shocked to see that she had been crying. She knew that grown-ups never, ever cried unless something really bad had happened.

"Sit down, please, Alice," Mr Gregory said. He was a big man with a sandy moustache and bushy eyebrows. He always wore suits made out of rough cloth that made Alice think of Shredded Wheat. His voice rumbled like a steamroller.

Alice sat down next to Alexa's Mum who reached out at once and squeezed her hand.

"I'm afraid, Alice, I have some very bad

news for you," Mr Gregory said. "Your mother and father boarded the plane to fly back to England last night. But it never arrived. It crashed shortly after take-off. There were no survivors. I'm so very, very sorry."

Alexa's Mum burst into tears as if it was the first time she had heard the news. Alice stared at her. She felt frozen inside, her mind unable to take in what she had been told.

The room seemed to float away from her, Mr Gregory's desk seeming to stretch and get wider.

The two adults seemed very remote. But Alice didn't feel anything at all.

# Chapter 3
# Aunt Vanessa

It was two days after her parents' funeral. Alice slept and ate and talked to people. They all said she was being very brave.

But everything still seemed like a dream. She had been taken back to her old house to pack up her belongings. She was going to live with her Aunt Vanessa in Cornwall.

The journey from Harrogate to Bodmin took almost an entire day. Alexa's Dad, Mr Pike, drove Alice down. Alexa came too, but she spent most of the journey moaning that she felt too hot or too cold or saying she was going to be sick. Alice spent most of the journey staring silently out of the window. She watched the countryside become wilder, more untamed. There were wide stretches of moorland covered in bracken and gorse. Now and again she drifted off to sleep.

It was dark when they reached Clagston, a village on the edge of Bodmin Moor. This is where her Aunt Vanessa lived. Alice had always liked her Mum's elder sister, though she wasn't sure whether she wanted to live with her. She wouldn't have minded if Aunt Vanessa had moved up to Harrogate to look after her, but Cornwall was such a long way away.

The cottages in Clagston were small and solid-looking. There weren't many streetlights, and anyway the darkness seemed blacker and stronger out here in the country, more savage somehow.

Aunt Vanessa's cottage was at the end of the village and was the last one you reached before the moor. Like all the others, it was a sturdy little building. A rambling rose climbed across the stonework. Its windows glowed in welcome.

As soon as Alice stepped out of the car, she smelt the gorse and bracken. She breathed it in until she felt dizzy. Then she helped Alexa's Dad carry her cases up the path to the front door. The door knocker was in the shape of a dog's head. Mr Pike gave it four short raps. He was standing up very straight as if he was someone important.

"One niece, safely delivered," he announced when Aunt Vanessa opened the door.

When she saw her Aunt, Alice felt tears spring to her eyes. Aunt Vanessa was stouter than Mum and not as pretty, but in that moment she looked so much like her that it brought home to Alice exactly what she had lost.

Alice dropped her suitcase and held up her arms like a baby. Aunt Vanessa stepped forward and hugged her. Alice noticed that her cardigan smelled of cinnamon and apples and wood smoke.

Alexa and her Dad left after supper. Alice was tired and she was glad to go to bed early.

"There, there, Alice," Aunt Vanessa said, as she tucked her up. "We'll look after each other, you and I. Don't you worry about a thing."

# Chapter 4
# Something In The Room

Her new room was pretty, with a little fireplace and a bay window which looked out over the moor. Aunt Vanessa had gone to so much trouble to make her feel welcome. There was a brightly-coloured quilt on the bed and a vase of flowers on the dressing table. On the floor beneath the window there was a beautiful doll's house filled with bits of furniture and little wooden people.

The smell of the flowers had reminded Alice of her parents' funeral, but she didn't tell Aunt Vanessa that. Her Aunt's house was nice, but it was strange and new. Everything was different to how it had been at home with Mum and Dad. Silly things like the toothpaste being a different brand to the one she normally used, or the boiler in the airing cupboard burbling like an old man with indigestion made her want to cry.

In spite of being tired after her long journey, it took Alice a long time to get to sleep. An hour or two later, she was suddenly awake again. She opened her eyes but could see nothing, hear nothing. And yet she sensed that someone was in the room with her. Someone or some*thing*.

Alice heard a snuffling sound and suddenly she felt something land on her legs. She wanted to scream, to jump up, but she was too terrified to move. She imagined a spider the size of a cat scuttling up her chest towards her face. She jerked out a hand to push it away and touched a furry body.

She realised then that it was one of her Aunt's dogs – Holly or Pip. The dogs were mongrels and were brother and sister. They had fox-like faces, but were short-haired and had stumpy legs. Their coats were white with brown blotches. They were friendly animals and their tails wagged constantly, lashing the legs of anyone who got too close.

Alice loved dogs, and having them around would be one of the good things about coming here to live with her Aunt. Dad had never let her have a dog. He had always said that their lives were too busy, that they wouldn't have time to take it for walks or look after it properly.

Earlier that evening, when Alice had been hugging Pip and giggling as he tried to lick her face, Aunt Vanessa had said, "Holly and Pip belong to you too now, Alice. You can play with them whenever you like. Dogs are very good at cheering you up when you're feeling a bit down."

The dog — Alice still didn't know which one it was — shuffled towards her. She could hear its wagging tail thumping the bed.

Then she felt a little tongue dart out and lick her face. Alice hugged the dog in the darkness. It was warm as a hot water bottle and snuggled into her like a baby.

Feeling safe and almost happy, Alice laid her head back on her pillow and drifted off to sleep.

# Chapter 5
# Missing

It was April, more than three months since her parents had died and Alice was beginning to settle into her new way of life.

The first few weeks had been hard. She had cried a lot for her Mum and Dad and had had to try and get used to new surroundings, a new school, a new life. Aunt Vanessa had been kind and patient, but

Alice knew that those early days had been hard for her too. Her Aunt had lived on her own for so long that she had become set in her ways. There had been times when the two of them had got on one another's nerves. At last, though, they had begun to get used to each other.

Although Alice still ached inside when she thought about her parents, she liked her new school and quickly became best friends with a girl called Natalie, whose parents owned a pottery in the village.

"Did you hear about Sally Marsden?" said Natalie one day. "She's gone missing."

"Missing?" Alice said. "What do you mean?"

"She went out on the moor yesterday after school with Zoe and Rachel. They were playing hide-and-seek. Sally went off to hide and the other two couldn't find her. They spent ages walking around on the moor, shouting her name. Then, as it was getting dark, they had to come home. Sally's parents called the police. But they haven't found her yet."

"When I looked out of my window this morning, I saw some policemen and a whole lot of other people spread out over the moor," said Alice, "I wondered what they were up to."

"My Dad went out to help look for her, but he said he couldn't imagine anyone being able to survive on the moor all night.

It was so cold and wet and there's no shelter up there," said Natalie in a hushed voice.

"Do you think she's dead, then?" said Alice.

"Could be."

"What do you think has happened to her?"

"Maybe she fell down a hole and broke her neck or something. My Dad says there's lots of old mine shafts on the moor. He says they used to mine tin around here. Or maybe someone murdered her."

Alice felt sick. She thought of her parents, of how they must have felt in the seconds before their plane had crashed. "Poor Sally," she whispered.

"I know," said Natalie, though her eyes sparkled with the excitement of it all, "it's awful, isn't it?"

# Chapter 6
# The Moor

"Natalie's Dad says that there are lots of old mine shafts on the moor. He says that Sally Marsden probably fell down one of them," Alice told her Aunt Vanessa that weekend.

Aunt Vanessa curled up her nose and shook her head. "Nonsense. The mines were mapped and filled in a long time ago."

The two of them had driven out to the coast as they did most weekends and were walking along a wind-swept beach. Holly and Pip were chasing each other round in circles, sometimes running up to the sea's edge and snapping at the foamy tide as it surged around their paws.

"What do you think happened to her, then?" Alice asked, as she pushed her long hair away from her face.

Her Aunt looked out to sea, lips pursed. After a moment she said, "The poor girl probably just wandered off and got lost. She'll turn up in the end, one way or another."

Alice secretly thought that if they were going to find her alive on the moor they would have done so by now. The search had been going on for three days. There had been policemen and local people and tracker dogs, even a helicopter.

"Maybe she was kidnapped," Alice said.

Aunt Vanessa frowned, "Who by?"

"Maybe whoever it was followed her from school," said Alice, "and waited until she was on her own." She had read a story like that in the newspaper.

Her Aunt glanced at her, her face set against the wind. "You are not to give yourself nightmares over this, Alice. Now let's find a nice tea shop and put all this out of our minds for a while."

They found a place that did thick ham sandwiches in home-baked bread and delicious chocolate cake. Afterwards they climbed back into Aunt Vanessa's battered old Range Rover and drove to Mousehole. They spent the afternoon poking around the antique shops and the craft galleries there.

When they got back it was dusk. The dogs ran into the cottage as soon as Aunt Vanessa opened the door. Pip raced up the stairs whilst Holly headed for the kitchen in search of a drink. Alice was halfway up the stairs when Pip began to bark.

"What's that silly dog yapping at now?"
Aunt Vanessa said.

"I'll go and see," offered Alice.

"Send him down for his dinner, would
you, dear? That'll shut him up."

Alice ran up the stairs. The sound of
Pip's barking was coming from her
bedroom. The dog sounded strange, his
barking fierce but high-pitched as if he was
frightened of something.

"What is it, Pip?" Alice asked, walking
into her bedroom.

Pip's body was rigid with tension. He
was standing with his back paws on the
roof of the doll's house, his front paws on

the windowsill. He was barking at something outside. His muzzle was pressed to the glass. The hair was standing up along his back and neck and his tail was as straight as an iron bar.

Alice walked up behind Pip and looked out of the window. The sky was the colour of dark blue denim. The moor was almost black beneath it.

Standing in the bracken on the moor was a small figure. It was wearing a school blazer and a skirt which flapped around its knees in the wind. Although it was too dark to see the figure's face, Alice felt that it was looking straight at her. A ripple of cold went through her body.

As Alice watched, the figure seemed to sink into the ground and disappear. The dark blue sky filled the area where it had stood. Pip whimpered and dived under the bed.

Alice yanked her curtains closed and stepped back from the window. She got down on all fours and looked under the. bed. Pip was curled up, trembling with fear. His eyes appeared too big for his face and were shining white in the shadows. Alice had to drag him out and all the way downstairs.

She said nothing to her Aunt. What was there to say?

# Chapter 7
## Lost

Three weeks after Sally Marsden disappeared, life was getting back to normal. The search for her was scaled down, although the case remained open. The newspaper reporters who had been hanging around in the village had drifted away. There weren't as many police officers around either. They had gone back to wherever they had come from.

While the full-scale search had been underway, Aunt Vanessa and Alice had stopped taking the dogs for their daily walk on the moors. As soon as things had become calmer, however, Aunt Vanessa was keen to get back to where they had left off. The first time she suggested this to Alice, Alice felt like saying no, she had too much homework. But then she thought that being in the cottage alone while her Aunt was out on the moor with the dogs would be even worse than going with her. So in the end she pulled on her boots and went out.

As they walked, Alice kept imagining she could hear something in the bracken whispering to her. She kept thinking she could see dark figures out of the corners of her eyes. But they were only trees and bushes when she turned to look at them.

She watched Pip closely at first, but the little dog seemed quite happy to be out on the moor, racing around with his sister as usual.

At last Alice lost sight of the dogs. This often happened. When they were playing, they would disappear for minutes at a time.

Alice had never told Aunt Vanessa about the figure she had seen on the moor and wasn't going to. Her Aunt was a no-nonsense kind of woman who had no time for "silly stories".

"Shouldn't we be getting back?" Alice said after they had been walking for about 45 minutes. She tried not to sound nervous, but she didn't like the way that the sky was beginning to grow dark and the wind was getting stronger.

Aunt Vanessa stopped and looked up. The wind rippled her coat across her back. Her face looked raw, her eyes were watery.

"I suppose so," she said. "We don't want to get caught in the rain, do we?"

She turned and led the way, sticking her fingers in her mouth and whistling for Holly and Pip. Alice expected to see the dogs running through the bracken or hear their answering barks. But there was neither sight nor sound of them.

"They'll catch us up," Aunt Vanessa said. "Come along."

The wind whipped up, stinging Alice's eyes, as the sky grew darker and shadows gathered on the land. Alice followed her Aunt, lowering her head to watch her feet. After ten minutes, she looked up into the wind and said, "I still haven't seen the dogs. Have you?"

Aunt Vanessa shook her head, then shouted, "Holly! Pip! Come here!"

There was no response. Alice thought of the dark figure she had seen from the window and how it had sunk into the moor.

"They probably can't hear me above the wind," Aunt Vanessa said. "Don't worry, dear, they know their way home."

It started to rain hard, the wind driving it into their faces. By the time they reached the cottage, Alice was bent almost double. Her face was numb and her head ached.

Once they were inside, Alice said, "What about Holly and Pip? We can't just leave them out there."

"Perhaps you'd like to go and look for them," Aunt Vanessa snapped, then shook her head. In a softer voice she said, "Don't worry, dear, they'll turn up. I expect they're sheltering somewhere."

But two hours passed and the dogs didn't come back, and now it was Aunt Vanessa who wanted to go and look for them, despite the dark and the rain. Alice, though, managed to make her see that it would be hopeless in these conditions, that they would do better to wait until morning.

It was after midnight when Alice went to bed, leaving her Aunt sitting by the fire, her face tight with worry. Alice had tried to get her to go up to bed too, but her Aunt had shaken her head and said, "No, I'll wait up for a bit, just in case."

The next morning Alice was woken up suddenly by the slamming of a door. She rolled over and looked at her clock and saw that it was 5:45 a.m. She threw off her covers, climbed out of bed and went to the window.

She saw the back of her Aunt's quilted jacket as she plodded out on to the moor. Alice felt sad for her when she saw the dogs' leads hanging loosely from her hand. Aunt Vanessa was a strong, practical woman, but she seemed lost without her dogs.

Alice wanted to tell her to wait so that they could look for the dogs together. Her fingers fumbled with the window latch, but by the time she managed to open the window, Aunt Vanessa was out of sight.

Now she would have to worry until her Aunt was safely home. That's if she *ever* comes back, a small voice whispered in her mind. Maybe she would disappear, just as Holly and Pip and Sally Marsden had done. If that happened, what would become of Alice? Would she be taken away and put into a home? The thought terrified her so much that she crawled back into her bed, pulled her covers over her head and prayed and prayed to God to keep her Aunt safe from whatever was out there on the moor.

# Chapter 8
# The Scratching

Her Aunt did come back. She had turned up at five to nine, just a few minutes before Alice should have arrived at school. Her face had been red and weary, her shoulders stooped. The dog leads had still been dangling from her pocket.

Seeing Alice running down the stairs in her pyjamas, she had been angry at first, wanting to know why the girl wasn't ready for school. Then she had seen the tears running down Alice's face and her anger disappeared.

"Whatever's the matter?" she had said gently as Alice had wrapped her arms around her and hugged her tightly.

Alice could hardly speak from crying. "I thought … you weren't … ever coming … back."

"Oh, Alice," her Aunt had said, stroking her hair, "I'll always be here for you. Always."

********

April slipped into May. Aunt Vanessa tried to put a brave face on the dogs' disappearance, though Alice knew she was a lot more upset than she was letting on. One night, Alice had woken and had heard her Aunt weeping downstairs. Alice had wanted to go to her, but she had been afraid to. She thought maybe her Aunt wouldn't want to be seen crying.

Now Alice had woken in the night again. This time she left her room and stood barefoot on the upstairs landing. The house was dark and silent. She was wearing her blue pyjamas with a picture of Casper the Friendly Ghost on the front. The air felt damp and smelt of bracken. Her fingers and toes were cold. There had been a lot of rain recently. It drummed on the moor till everything was soaking wet. Then the wind blew over it making ripples like waves on the sea.

Alice decided to go down the stairs. She didn't know why she'd woken up, or even why she was going downstairs – she just felt as though she ought to.

The stairs creaked as she stepped on them, but the sound seemed muffled, as if her ears were full of cotton wool. As soon as she entered the lounge, though, her ears unblocked and she heard the scratching.

It was hard to tell where the sound was coming from, but it seemed very loud. She decided that it was coming from the kitchen and she walked towards the door on the far side of the room.

She went into the kitchen and switched on the light. The dog leads were still hanging on the hook above the fridge. Her Aunt's muddy green Wellingtons stood on sheets of the *Daily Telegraph*, with their toes pointing towards the back door. Ever since the dogs went missing, Aunt Vanessa had been out searching the moor every day. She always said she was just going out, but Alice knew she spent the time looking for Holly and Pip.

Alice glanced at the kitchen window which looked out on to the moor, but saw nothing but black beyond the glass. Suddenly she was scared of what might come to the window and peer in at her, and so she looked away.

She heard the scratching noise again. This time Alice knew that it was coming from the other side of the back door. She didn't know why, but all at once she felt sure that the dogs had finally found their way home. She imagined herself going into her Aunt's bedroom and saying, *Aunt Vanessa, look what I've found,* and then seeing the joy on her Aunt's face when the dogs rushed in, tails wagging, as they leaped up on to the bed.

Full of excitement, she undid the bolts on the back door and turned the key. Then she grabbed the handle and pulled the door open.

Sally Marsden stood there. She had obviously been dead for some time.

Her face was purple and slimy-looking, like rotten meat. Her clothes and hair were covered with dirt and bits of bracken. Insects were crawling on her — earwigs and fat red centipedes. She smelled so bad that Alice staggered back as if she had been punched in the stomach, her foot clanging down on something metallic.

It was one of the dog bowls, which had never been put away. It skidded away from under her foot and she fell over backwards. She hit the floor so hard that her breath rushed out of her lungs.

As Sally Marsden shuffled into the house, rotting hands reaching towards her, Alice closed her eyes and tried to scream.

Then she felt strong hands grab her arms trying to drag them away from her face. Far away, through her panic, Alice heard her Aunt shouting her name over and over.

Alice stopped trying to scream. Her Aunt's voice was right beside her, yelling into her ear. She opened her eyes.

It was Aunt Vanessa's hands which were gripping her wrists, her Aunt's frightened face which was looking down at her. Alice went limp and began to shiver. She collapsed into her Aunt's arms. Now all she could smell was heather and bracken as the cold wind swirled in through the open back door.

# Chapter 9

# The Police Station, Part 2

The icy blue room where Alice was sitting with the two police officers fell silent as she reached this stage in her story. Alice stopped talking, as if the memories were too agonising for her. She stared down at the table.

Detective Inspector Farrington glanced at Detective Sergeant Lockwood, then at the tape recorder. She sat back in her creaking orange chair and said, "Would you like a break, Alice?"

Alice looked up, her eyes staring. Either she hadn't slept for a long time or she was drugged up, Farrington couldn't tell which. The girl looked surprised by the question.

"No," she said, "no, I ... I was just thinking, trying to work out the next thing that happened. I suppose nothing did, really, for years, until a few weeks ago. And then ..."

"Then what, Alice?" said Farrington softly.

"Well, you know ... what happened."

"I want to hear it from you," said Farrington.

"Well," said Alice, "I suppose *something* happened in those years. Sally Marsden was never found. Her parents got divorced because of the stress of it all and in the end they moved away from the area. I went on having nightmares about her for a while, but none were as bad as that first time. I didn't sleepwalk again. After a bit, a year or two, I stopped being scared of the moor and by the time I was thirteen, fourteen, I even started going out there with my friends, just to smoke and hang out and get away from things, you know."

"By 'things', you mean your Aunt?" said Farrington.

Alice shrugged. "I suppose so. I mean, we got on OK, but it was a teenage thing, you know? She was very protective of me and a bit lonely and I just wanted more freedom to go out and be with my friends."

"You wanted to spread your wings a bit?" said Farrington.

"Yeah."

"And she wouldn't let you?" said Lockwood.

"She couldn't really stop me, but she didn't like it."

"Did you used to argue?" Lockwood asked.

"Sometimes. Not all the time. Sometimes we had a laugh together. She was OK."

"We have one witness who overheard you in the pub threatening to kill your Aunt," said Farrington.

"God, I didn't *mean* it," said Alice. "Everyone says that about the people they love, don't they? You hear parents saying it about their kids all the time. 'I'll bloody kill him when he gets home', they say. They're not serious though. I'd never have done anything bad to my Aunt. I loved her. She was like a Mum to me."

"So what happened a few weeks ago?" asked Farrington.

"I was just about to take my A levels. It was a Saturday morning and I was upstairs revising." Alice paused.

"What is it?" asked Farrington.

"Well ... this is where it all starts to get really weird. This is the bit you're not going to believe."

# Chapter 10
# The Miracle

"Alice!" Aunt Vanessa screamed up the stairs. "Alice!"

Alice jumped, then felt her heart sink. She put down her pen. *God*, she thought, *what have I done now?*

She hauled herself off the bed, switched off her CD player and went out onto the landing. She leaned over the banister. "What is it?" she called.

Her Aunt appeared at the bottom of the stairs. She looked strange, her eyes were wide, her skin pale. Her voice too was odd. "Would you come down here a minute, please?"

"Why?" asked Alice, annoyed to be interrupted.

"Just come down, please."

"I'm busy revising," insisted Alice.

"It won't take a moment."

Aunt Vanessa disappeared into the kitchen before Alice could say any more.

Alice sighed and trudged down the stairs, wondering what her Aunt wanted. Maybe she had found the condoms in her jacket pocket. Worse, her Aunt might have looked in her purse and discovered the photo of her and her boyfriend, Paul, naked together.

Alice felt herself getting angry. If that was the case, she'd ask what right her Aunt had to go through her things. For God's sake, she was eighteen now, she wasn't a little girl any more. What she got up to with Paul was her own business.

She stomped into the lounge, ready for a fight.

"I'm here," Aunt Vanessa called from the kitchen.

Alice walked towards the door, expecting to find her Aunt holding her jacket in one hand, a packet of condoms in the other.

She walked into the kitchen and stopped dead. She couldn't believe what she was seeing. For a moment the world seemed to tilt. Her head swam.

Aunt Vanessa was standing in the middle of the kitchen floor. There was joy and disbelief on her face. Sitting calmly at her feet, looking exactly as they had done when they had disappeared nine years earlier, were Holly and Pip.

Alice's voice was weak. "What's going on?"

Her Aunt smiled, tears in her eyes. "They've come back," she whispered.

Alice stared at the dogs. They stared back at her coldly. "But ... they can't have!" she said. "It's impossible!"

Aunt Vanessa crouched down and hugged first Holly and then Pip. The dogs just sat there, still staring at Alice with a watchful expression. "See for yourself," her Aunt whispered. "Look at what's right here in front of us."

"It's a trick," said Alice, but even as she said it she knew that it was not. To non-dog owners, dogs of the same breed all look identical. To the trained eye, they all look different, just as people do. These dogs did not just look like Holly and Pip, they *were* Holly and Pip. There was no doubt about it.

And yet the whole thing *was* impossible. When Holly and Pip had disappeared they had been four years old, which meant that they were now both thirteen. In dog terms that was old and yet they appeared as lively as they had ever been. There was not even a trace of grey in either of their muzzles.

"Of course it's not a trick," said Aunt Vanessa softly. "It's a miracle, that's what it is. A miracle."

# Chapter 11
# Watching

Alice soon discovered that although the dogs looked the same, their characters and behaviour were quite different. She found this very disturbing. But Aunt Vanessa said that the poor things were probably just tired and suffering from shock.

It didn't seem like shock to Alice, though. The dogs had no fear in them. In fact, they seemed almost sly in their behaviour. They did what they were told, which kept her Aunt happy, but never showed any affection. They didn't race about like they used to, wagging their tails. They moved slowly and silently, like ghosts.

Aunt Vanessa put this down to the fact that they were no longer puppies, but Alice couldn't help feeling that it was more than that.

Sometimes they would creep up to her, appearing so suddenly and silently that they made her jump. It was almost as though they were doing it on purpose, to frighten her.

What was more, she couldn't help thinking that the dogs were watching her every move. She tried to tell herself that she was being silly, but even when the dogs were asleep she felt as though their eyes were on her.

Aunt Vanessa refused to talk about where the dogs might have been for the last nine years. All that mattered to her was that her beloved dogs were back.

"Don't you think we should tell someone?" Alice said one day.

"Tell who?" replied Aunt Vanessa.

Alice wanted to say "the police", but that would have sounded ridiculous. "I don't know ... the vet. Maybe he ought to look them over, check that they're healthy."

"Of course they're healthy," Aunt Vanessa said. "Anyone can see that."

"Yeah, but ... they never want to go for walks any more. They spend all their time just lying around."

"They're *old*," her Aunt chuckled. "Like me. Now, let's hear no more about it. The matter is closed."

# Chapter 12
# By The Light Of The Moon

When Alice woke up that night, it was as though she had gone back in time. For a few seconds she was a scared little girl again who had just arrived to live with her Aunt and was certain that something was in the room with her.

Then she came back to the present, sat up and pushed aside the covers. The cool air dried the sweat on her arms and legs and made her skin tingle. She was surprised to see that her curtains were wide open. The moor was staring in at her with one shining white eye.

It was the moon, of course. Its light leaked on to the moor, forming a milky crust. Alice wondered who had opened her curtains. Had she forgotten to close them? No, she couldn't believe that. Although the moor no longer frightened her, she still closed her curtains before it got dark. It had become a habit.

She looked around her moonlit room. She seemed to be alone. She licked her lips and realised she was thirsty. She swung her legs from the bed and put her feet on the floor.

Suddenly, something furry and fleshy came out from under the bed and slid against her calves. Alice screamed and pulled up her legs quickly.

It was one of the dogs. It slid round in front of her, its muzzle curled back over its teeth as if it was grinning. Its eyes seemed to shine yellow in the moonlight. It made no sound at all. It did not even seem to be breathing.

"What do you want?" croaked Alice.

The dog just stared at her. In some ways Alice would have felt better if it had growled or snarled.

"What do you want?" she said again, trying not to sound scared.

The dog stared at her for a moment longer, then turned and slid through the gap of the half-open door.

Alice shivered, then jumped up to shut the door, pressing her weight against it until it clicked. She switched on the light and got down on hands and knees to look under the bed. She had to make sure that she was now really alone. Her throat was dry with fear, but she was not going to leave her room tonight, not for anything.

Instead, to quench her thirst, she crossed to the window and licked the condensation from the glass.

# Chapter 13
# The Skins

Alice's boyfriend, Paul, had long hair, drove a purple Spitfire, played bass guitar in a local band, wore bangles on his wrist and a large, gold loop in his left ear.

Aunt Vanessa didn't like Paul, but then she had never liked any of Alice's boyfriends. It was odd really, because before Alice's parents had died, her Aunt had been perfectly happy to live alone. Now, though, it was as if she thought every man Alice met was going to take her away. Even her last boyfriend, poor old Roger, who was polite, smart and well-spoken, had not been accepted.

Alice hoped that things would be different now that the dogs were back. In spite of what she thought of them, she had to admit that they had returned at a good time as far as she was concerned. In five months she would be going to university and she didn't want to be made to feel guilty for leaving her Aunt on her own. Now she would have the dogs for company.

It was Saturday night. Alice and Paul had been for a pizza, seen a film and finished up at the pub. Now Paul was driving her home, his Spitfire roaring through the country lanes.

"Do you want to come in for a coffee?" she asked when they pulled up in front of the cottage.

He shrugged his shoulders. "Nah, I'm cool. I'll see you tomorrow."

"She might have gone to bed," said Alice.

"Yeah, but if she hasn't she'll just get us tense and I don't want that after the night we've just had."

"No, me neither. All right, I'll see you tomorrow."

She leaned across the seat to kiss him and pulled back ten minutes later, her face flushed.

Paul grinned. "You coming to the gig tomorrow?"

"Course I am. I'll be there with my big stick, beating off the groupies."

His grin became a laugh. "Oh yeah, as if."

She kissed him again and got out of the car. The Spitfire roared like a lion before speeding away. Alice stood at the gate, waving, then turned towards the cottage.

She half-expected her Aunt's face to be peering at her through the curtains. It had happened before. She would enter the cottage and her Aunt would say something like, *I just looked out to see what that terrible row was. I thought it must be joyriders, all that noise.*

Tonight, though, there was no sign of Aunt Vanessa. Either she hadn't heard Paul's car or she had gone to bed. Or she's fussing round the dogs, Alice thought and wondered again whether she was being paranoid about them.

A couple of times, when she was out with Paul or her friends, Alice had almost managed to convince herself that she was wrong about Pip and Holly. However, each time she had gone back to the cottage and had come into contact with them again, her worries came flooding back. Their presence seemed to poison the atmosphere around them. They were like the rotten apples in the barrel, turning everything else bad.

Alice unlocked the door and went inside. She walked into the lounge. The lights were on and there was a fire burning low in the grate, but there was no sign of Aunt Vanessa. Alice couldn't hear her moving about upstairs, so guessed that she must be asleep. It was odd, though, that she had not put the fireguard in place as she always did before she went up to bed.

Alice went through to the kitchen to make herself a cup of tea. She braced herself to meet the dogs, who would no doubt stare at her from their baskets beside the back door.

When she turned on the light, however, she saw that their baskets were empty. She looked around, thinking that they might be hiding, but there was nowhere else in the room the dogs could be. Perhaps they're sleeping with Aunt Vanessa, she thought. Or perhaps they're in *my* room, hiding under the bed, waiting for me to come back.

She wanted to rush upstairs and check. Instead, she finished making her tea. She told herself firmly that she wasn't going to let them get to her. All the same, as she carried her tea upstairs, her heart was pumping hard.

The door to her room was slightly open. She stood outside for a moment, listening, but heard nothing. Even the wind was quiet tonight.

At last she pushed at the door. It swung open with a creak. Alice stepped inside and switched on the light.

She looked quickly around. Everything seemed normal. She put her mug on the dressing table. Then she crouched down and looked under the bed. The dogs were not there. Neither were they in the wardrobe, nor on the windowsill behind the curtain. Unless her Aunt had taken the dogs out, therefore, they *must* be sleeping with her in her room.

Alice was glad that the dogs had chosen

to sleep with her Aunt. Rather her than me, she thought. She picked up her mug of tea and flopped onto the bed. Then she frowned. There was something under the bedclothes, something soft but a bit bulky, like a rolled-up sweater.

She got up off the bed and looked down. Sure enough, there was a hump in the bed. It must be her nightshirt, though normally she folded that up and put it under her pillow. Sighing, she pulled back the bedclothes.

At first she was not sure what she was looking at. It appeared to be a small rug of animal fur rolled into a ball. She lifted it up and unrolled it and realised that it was not one rug but two, rolled up tightly together.

The rugs, if that was what they were, were tiny. They were white with brown blotches.

All at once, Alice went cold with shock and stepped back, throwing the things on to the bed. They were not rugs, they were skins and what was more they looked like the skins of her Aunt's two dogs. But how could that be? The skins were not fresh, not bloody, but dry and smooth on the inside. Alice could see the eye-holes, the ears, the toes. Suddenly she felt horribly sick and she turned round, her head spinning.

She tore open the door to her room and tried to call her Aunt's name, but only a whisper came out. She ran towards the room at the other end of the corridor, feeling as if she was going to fall at any moment. The walls seemed to sway around her. Blood roared in her ears. The door to her Aunt's room was open a crack, as hers had been. Alice reached out and pushed it hard.

There was not much light, but Alice could just make out that her Aunt was lying on the bed. She saw with horror that her Aunt's legs, white and fat, were streaked with something that looked black in the darkness, but which Alice knew was blood. There was a strange sound in the room, like an animal feeding. Alice tried to make out the rest of her Aunt's body and realised that something pink and shiny was hunched over her.

Alice must have made some sound, because the creature, whatever it was, suddenly turned to look at her. It was skinny and evil-looking. Its flesh was pink and slimy like an earthworm's. It had a sharp, little snout in a flat head and its eyes were beady and black like a spider's. It opened a tiny mouth, showing rows of needle-sharp teeth and snarled at her. Its muzzle was dripping with blood.

The creature moved away from the bed and Alice caught a glimpse of her Aunt's upper body. It was torn and shredded. The bed sheets, even the carpet, were soaked with blood.

Stunned by the horror of the scene, Alice could only stand and stare for several seconds. It was only when the creature began to totter towards her on spindly legs that she was able to move. Just before she turned and fled, Alice saw a second creature on the other side of the bed. It stared at her for a moment and then, with apparent enjoyment, dipped its snout and continued feasting.

# Chapter 14
# The Police Station, Part 3

In the interview room in the police station, there was silence. Alice hung her head, hands clenched tightly together. Farrington looked at Lockwood and raised her eyebrows. Lockwood shook his head and smiled.

"Alice," Farrington said. The girl did not respond. "Alice," she repeated, more sharply.

This time Alice looked up, flinching as though she had been slapped.

"Alice, do you really believe that what you've told us is the truth?"

Alice looked confused for a moment, then nodded and whispered, "Yes."

"Then why didn't you tell someone before? Why didn't you come to the police straight away? Why have you been on the run for two weeks, travelling around the country, sleeping rough?"

"I don't know ... I ... *you* didn't see them. Those things were ... *evil.* I felt as though they'd marked me out. I thought that they'd find me wherever I went and the only thing I could do was to keep moving."

"Didn't you think that the police would protect you?" Farrington asked.

"I didn't know if you could."

"Didn't it occur to you that running away would make it look like you were guilty and that we would catch you in the end?"

Alice stared at her. Her eyes were bloodshot, her hair dirty. "I haven't done anything. I'm not guilty."

"Aren't you?"

"No."

"Didn't you kill your Aunt and then dump her body on the moor before going on the run?"

"*No!* You can't believe that! You must have seen what those things did to her," Alice shouted suddenly.

"The body was not found for several days," continued Farrington, "and when it was ... well, there are a large number of animals and birds out on that moor. They could all have had a go at it."

"No, I didn't kill her! The dogs killed her! It wasn't me!"

Alice began to sob, her body shuddering. Farrington stared at her for a moment and then said, "I think we'll call it a day for now. We're going to have to detain you, Alice. We'll continue this in the morning."

Farrington leaned forward and placed her hand on the STOP button of the tape recorder. "Interview concluded at 4:42 a.m., Friday, 26th May 2000."

# Chapter 15
# The Cell

An hour later, Detective Inspector Farrington was ready to go home. She was exhausted, but knew she would only have time to grab three, maybe four hours' sleep. Then she had to be back at the station to question Alice Manly again.

Five forty-five a.m. was the dead hour before dawn and the station was quiet. The nightclubs were closed, the drunks were sleeping it off in their cells and the morning shift had yet to report for duty.

Farrington yawned and reached for her coat. After Alice had been taken down to the cells, she'd had a brief chat with Lockwood. He had been convinced that the girl was off her rocker. Farrington had retreated to her office with a cup of tea to think things through. She wanted to be as clear-headed as possible before she spoke to Alice again. She couldn't help thinking that the girl was at least telling the truth as she saw it. Unless Alice Manly was a brilliant actress, she was clearly terrified of something.

Farrington locked her office door behind her and headed down the corridor towards the station entrance. As she passed the connecting corridor that led down to the cells, she glanced in that direction.

At that precise moment the screaming started.

It was shrill and raw and full of absolute, awful terror. Farrington went rigid with shock for a moment, as if she'd had a bucket of iced water thrown over her. Then she set off running, down the stairs to the cell area. Her feet moved so fast that she was in danger of falling headlong. As she reached the bottom, the screaming choked into silence.

The corridor which contained the cells was narrow with a low ceiling. It was lit with fluorescent light. There were twelve cells in all, six on each side. Alice Manly was in cell number four.

Farrington ran up to the thick, metal door and put her eye to the spy-hole. However all she could see was blackness.

"Alice," she said sharply. "Alice, can you hear me?"

What she heard in response made her rear back from the door in surprise, her heart thumping hard. The sound coming from inside the cell did not seem human. Farrington leaned forward to listen again, but at that moment the sound of heavy boots coming down the metal staircase from above drowned it out.

She stepped back from the door as a uniformed sergeant appeared with a bunch of keys. As the key turned in the lock, Farrington felt her body tensing up. She wondered whether what she had heard on the other side could really have been the snarling of an animal.

The door swung open and for one fleeting moment, Farrington felt something squeeze past her, brushing against her leg. Then she let out a gasp of horror as the sergeant switched on the light in the cell.

Barrington Stoke would like to thank all its readers for commenting on the manuscript before publication and in particular:

Kim Beaton
Kate Berry
Hugh Caldwell
Eddie Chan
Tom Crabbe
Jack Davidson
Richard Fabri
Ashleigh Findlay
Mark Grant
Valerie Higson
Valerie Hirst
Caroline Holden
Shelley Kyle

James Lawson
Kenny Li
Cheryleigh Niven
Gemma Pearson
Dorothy Porter
Claire Ripak
Jocelyn Scott
Stacey Shields
Helen Spence
Liz Watson
Lesley Ann Wilson
Hayley Winter

## Become a Consultant!

Would you like to give us feedback on our titles before they are published?  Contact us at the email address below – we'd love to hear from you!

Email: info@barringtonstoke.co.uk
Website: www.barringtonstoke.co.uk

If you loved this book why don't you read ...

## The Cold Heart of Summer

### by Alan Gibbons

ISBN 1-842990-80-2

"... the face was screaming. It was an awful, silent scream."

Debbie knows the stories about Old Man Sexton who haunts the Grange: the big, old house on the hill. But a house can't be evil, can it?

When her father starts working at the Grange, Debbie's feelings tell a different story. Outside the house it is summer, but inside it is bitter, cold winter. Can Debbie make her father listen before it is too late?

You can order *The Cold Heart of Summer* directly from our website at
**www.barringtonstoke.co.uk**